The Tale of the
Flopsy Bunnies

FREDERICK WARNE
Published by the Penguin Group
Penguin Books Ltd., 80 Strand, London WC2R 0RL, England
Penguin Group (USA) Inc., 375 Hudson Street, New York, New York 10014, USA
Penguin Group (Australia), 250 Camberwell Road,
Camberwell, Victoria 3124, Australia (a division of Pearson Australia Group Pty. Ltd.)
Penguin Group (Canada), 90 Eglinton Avenue East, Suite 700, Toronto,
Ontario M4P 2Y3, Canada (a division of Pearson Penguin Canada Inc.)
Penguin Books India Pvt. Ltd., 11 Community Centre,
Panchsheel Park, New Delhi 110 017, India
Penguin Group (NZ), 67 Apollo Drive, Rosedale, Auckland 0632,
New Zealand (a division of Pearson New Zealand Ltd.)
Penguin Books (South Africa) (Pty.)
Ltd, 24 Sturdee Avenue, Rosebank, Johannesburg 2196, South Africa

Penguin Books Ltd., Registered Offices: 80 Strand, London WC2R 0RL, England

www.peterrabbit.com

001 – 10 9 8 7 6 5 4 3 2 1

With thanks to Ruth Palmer.
Manufactured in China.

ISBN 978-0-7232-6837-6

The Tale of the
Flopsy Bunnies

based on the original tale by
BEATRIX POTTER™

F. WARNE & CO

An Imprint of Penguin Group (USA) Inc.

It is said that eating too much lettuce makes one drowsy.

It certainly had a very drowsy effect upon the Flopsy Bunnies!

When Benjamin Bunny grew up, he married his cousin
Flopsy. They had a large family, and they were very
carefree and cheerful.

Since there was not always quite enough to eat, Benjamin used to take cabbages from Flopsy's brother, Peter Rabbit, who kept a nursery garden. Sometimes Peter Rabbit had no cabbages to spare.

When this happened, the Flopsy Bunnies went across the field
to a rubbish heap in the ditch outside Mr. McGregor's garden.

Mr. McGregor's rubbish heap was a mixture of jam jars,
paper bags, mountains of chopped grass from the mowing
machine (which always tasted oily), some rotten squashes,
and an old boot or two.

One day—oh joy!—there was lots of unattended lettuce which had flowered.

The Flopsy Bunnies simply stuffed themselves with lettuce. Little by little, one after another, they became very sleepy and lay down in the mown grass.

Benjamin was not as overcome as his children. Before going to sleep, he was awake enough to put a paper bag over his head to keep off the flies.

The little Flopsy Bunnies slept delightfully in the warm sun. From the lawn beyond the garden came the distant clackety sound of the mower. The bluebottle flies buzzed about the wall, and a little old mouse picked over the rubbish among the jam jars.

She was called Thomasina Tittlemouse, and she was a wood mouse with a long tail.

She rustled across the paper bag and woke
Benjamin Bunny.

The mouse apologized over and over and
said she knew Benjamin's cousin Peter Rabbit.

    While she and Benjamin were talking close to the wall,
they heard heavy footsteps above their heads. Suddenly
Mr. McGregor emptied out a sack of mown grass right
on top of the sleeping Flopsy Bunnies! Benjamin shrank
down under his paper bag. The mouse hid in a jam jar.

The little rabbits smiled sweetly in their sleep under the shower of grass; they did not wake up because the lettuce had made them so drowsy.

They dreamed that their mother, Flopsy, was tucking them in a hay bed.

Mr. McGregor looked down after emptying his sack. He saw some funny little brown tips sticking up through the grass.

He stared at them for some time.

After a while, a fly settled on one of them and it moved. It was an ear!

Mr. McGregor climbed down onto the rubbish heap.

"One, two, three, four! Five! Six little rabbits!" he said as he dropped the bunnies into his sack.

The Flopsy Bunnies dreamed their mother was turning them over in bed. They stirred a little in their sleep, but still they did not wake up.

Mr. McGregor tied up the sack and left it on the grass.

He went to put away the mower.

While he was gone, Mrs. Flopsy Bunny, who
had stayed home, came across the field. She
looked suspiciously at the sack and wondered
where everybody was.

Then the mouse came out of her jam jar, and
Benjamin took the paper bag off his head, and
they told her the sad story.

Benjamin and Flopsy were in despair because
they could not undo the string.

But Mrs. Tittlemouse was a resourceful person.
She nibbled a hole in the bottom corner of the sack.
The little rabbits were pulled out and
pinched awake.

Their parents stuffed the empty sack with three rotten squashes, an old boot brush, and two decayed turnips.

Then they all hid under a bush and watched for Mr. McGregor.

Mr. McGregor came back and picked up the sack and carried it off. He carried it hanging down as if it were heavy.

The Flopsy Bunnies followed at a safe distance. They watched him go into his house.

And then they crept up to the window to listen.

Mr. McGregor threw down the sack on the stone floor in a way that would have been extremely painful to the Flopsy Bunnies if they had been inside.

They could hear him drag his chair on the floor and chuckle, "One, two, three, four, five, six little rabbits!"

"Eh? What's that? What have they been eating now?" asked Mrs. McGregor.

"One, two, three, four, five, six fat little rabbits!" repeated Mr. McGregor, counting on his fingers. "One, two, three—"

"Don't be silly. What do you mean, you silly old man?"

"In the sack! One, two, three, four, five, six!" replied Mr. McGregor.

The youngest Flopsy Bunny jumped upon the windowsill.

Mrs. McGregor took the sack and felt it. She said she could feel six, but they must be *old* rabbits because they were so hard and all different shapes.

"Not fit to eat, but the skins will do fine to line my old cloak," she said.

"Line your old cloak?" shouted Mr. McGregor. "I shall sell them and buy myself tobacco!"

Mrs. McGregor untied the sack and put her hand inside. When she felt the vegetables, she became very, very angry. She said that Mr. McGregor had "done it on purpose."

And Mr. McGregor was very angry, too. He threw one of the rotten squashes through the kitchen window and hit the youngest Flopsy Bunny.

It was rather hurt.

Then Benjamin and Flopsy thought it was time to go home.

So Mr. McGregor did not get his tobacco, and Mrs. McGregor did not get her rabbit skins.

But that Christmas, Thomasina Tittlemouse got a present of enough rabbit wool to make herself a cloak and a hood and a handsome muff and a pair of warm mittens.

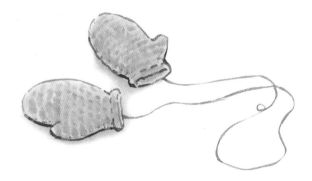